The Magic Key

Floppy and the Puppies

OXFORD

UNIVERSITY PRESS

Gran wanted a pet, so all the children went to the pet shop to help her choose one. Gran gave Floppy a bone to keep him happy while they looked around.

The shop was full of cute and cuddly animals like rabbits and chinchillas, but Gran had spotted the pet she wanted – a great big snake!

'Err, are you sure, Gran?' asked Chip nervously.

'Absolutely!' replied Gran.

Floppy walked over to the snake's tank and had a look in.

I do wish she'd at least choose a pet without fangs, he thought.

The key on Floppy's collar started to glow.

Suddenly, Chip, Gran, and Floppy were sucked into a vortex of dazzling colours and lights. They were whizzing round and round, faster and faster . . .

They found themselves by an old bungalow. As they looked around, a cat appeared.

'I'm Cutesy Kit,' it said. 'If you're looking for Mrs Barking, she's up there.'

Gran, Chip, and Floppy walked over to the bungalow – but not before Cutesy Kit had taken a swipe at Floppy! Not as cutesy as she looks, if you ask me, thought Floppy.

Brenda Barking was on the roof of the bungalow, feeding the squirrels. When she saw Chip and Gran approaching she climbed down her ladder to meet them.

'Welcome to my animal rescue centre. I see you've brought me a poor little stray dog,' she said, looking at Floppy. She took Floppy into the bungalow, followed by Gran and Chip.

In the kitchen, Brenda showed them two adorable looking puppies.
'I'm Tom,' said the first puppy. 'It's so nice to meet you.'
'And I'm Dick,' said the second one.
Brenda looked at Floppy. 'I shall call you Harry,' she said. Floppy wasn't too happy about that idea!
Brenda stroked Tom and Dick. 'Harry will have a marvellous time with them until I find him a new home,' she said.
'A new home!' cried Chip in alarm.

Brenda turned to walk out of the door. 'You have a look around. I'll be with you in a minute,' she said.

As soon as she'd left, Chip turned to Gran. 'We can't leave Floppy,' he said.

'We're not going to,' Gran reassured him. 'We'll be back after we've seen the other animals.'

As soon as they were alone, Tom and Dick transformed from cute puppies to snarling beasts!

'Give us your bone,' growled Tom, edging towards Floppy.

'Drop it, Slobbychops,' snarled Dick, showing his sharp teeth. Floppy was frightened, so he dropped his bone and crept away.

Tom and Dick immediately began gnawing at the bone. Dick bit it in half so they could have a piece each and Tom grabbed his half and tossed it above his head. The bone flew through the air and knocked a pie right off the kitchen table – and onto Floppy's head!

Just then, Brenda came back into the kitchen. She looked around at all the mess. 'What in the world has been going on in here?' she cried.

Tom and Dick were immediately transformed back into cute puppies.

'It's Harry,' said Dick, wide-eyed. 'He just started throwing his bone about.' Floppy's jaw dropped with amazement. Surely Brenda wasn't going to believe them!

Brenda took a rope out of her pocket and turned to Floppy.

'There's only one thing to do with a dog like you!' she said, and tied him to a pipe on the wall. Floppy whimpered – he couldn't believe what was happening!

'Right!' said Brenda. 'I'll go and fetch a muzzle to stop him doing any more damage.' And she walked out of the door.

Meanwhile, Chip and Gran had been looking around at the different animals. They found a tank with a snake curled up in it. 'Oh, aren't you beautiful,' said Gran.

'Beautiful?' snorted Brenda, as she walked past. 'That horrid thing! I call him slimy Simon.'

'But he isn't slimy at all,' said Gran. 'And I bet he's got a lovely nature.'

Brenda shook her head. 'Yesterday when I left him with the pups, he wrecked the kitchen!'

As soon as Brenda was out of earshot, the snake looked up at Gran. 'I didn't do it,' he said. 'But Mrs Barking believes everything the puppies say because they look so sweet.'

Gran took the snake out of his tank and he wrapped himself around her.

Gran turned to Chip. 'Come on,' she said. 'We're going to see what those puppies are up to!'

The puppies certainly weren't being very sweet at that moment! Tom and Dick had pulled all the food off the kitchen table and on to the floor. Then they chewed through Floppy's rope, to make it look as if he'd made the mess.

Floppy went and cowered under the table. He was fed up!

'Those little monsters!' cried Gran, as she and Chip looked through the kitchen window. 'I'm going to rescue Floppy!'

But Chip stopped her. 'No, Gran,' he said. 'Mrs Barking thinks those puppies are sweet. She's got to see what they're really like or she'll blame Floppy!'

So they called Brenda over to see with her own eyes what her puppies were up to.

Brenda was horrified at what she saw. Dick was chomping his way through a whole roast chicken, and Tom was chasing a terrified Floppy round and round the kitchen table!

Brenda, Gran, and Chip marched into the kitchen. 'Hold it right there!' Brenda shouted.

Tom and Dick were once again transformed into lovable little puppies. 'Look what he's done!' said Dick, looking at Floppy. 'We couldn't stop him.'

But Brenda had seen what the puppies were really like. She grabbed Tom and put the muzzle on him, and then she took Dick and tied him up to the water pipe. 'That'll teach you a lesson,' she said.

Brenda took the snake from Gran and then she gave Floppy a
big bone.

'If ever a dog deserved an enormous bone, it's you,' she said.

Chip and Gran looked at Floppy. 'The key's glowing,' said Chip.

We're going, thought Floppy.

Back at the pet shop, Mrs Robinson and the other children were waiting outside. Chip and Floppy walked out with Gran, who had an enormous snake wrapped around her.

'Good heavens,' gasped Mrs Robinson.

'I think I'll call him Simon,' said Gran.

'Don't worry,' said Chip to the others. 'He's not as scary as he looks.'

Gran climbed on to her motorbike. 'Let's all go home so you can get to know him properly,' she said. Then she turned to Simon. 'Who's a pretty boy then?' she said with a smile.

OXFORD
UNIVERSITY PRESS

Great Clarendon Street, Oxford OX2 6DP

Oxford University Press is a department of the University of Oxford.
It furthers the University's objective of excellence in research, scholarship,
and education by publishing worldwide in

Oxford New York

Athens Auckland Bangkok Bogotá Buenos Aires Calcutta
Cape Town Chennai Dar es Salaam Delhi Florence Hong Kong Istanbul
Karachi Kuala Lumpur Madrid Melbourne Mexico City Mumbai
Nairobi Paris São Paulo Shanghai Singapore Taipei Tokyo Toronto Warsaw

with associated companies in Berlin Ibadan

Oxford is a registered trade mark of Oxford University Press in the UK and in certain other countries